BOOK 4

Freddy Buttons

and the
Strawberry Patch Puzzle

Written by Fiona Dillon

Illustrated by Derry Dillon

About the Author

Fiona Dillon has a pet. It's not a cat. It's not a dog. It's a goose. A gander to be exact. He follows her everywhere. He even eats out of her hand! Fiona has a garden just like the one at Tumbledown Cottage. Collecting eggs in the garden is her favourite thing to do. Her second most favourite thing is to sit in the strawberry patch and eat the strawberries. She writes books for grown-ups too at **www.fionadillon.com** but what she really loves is writing about Freddy Buttons and his animal friends at **www.freddybuttons.com**.

Published by
Orpen Press
Lonsdale House
Avoca Avenue
Blackrock
Co. Dublin
Ireland
email: info@orpenpress.com
www.orpenpress.com
© Text: Fiona Dillon, 2015
Illustrations: Derry Dillon, 2015

ISBN 978-1-909895-86-7

Printed by Castuera Industrias Graficas, Spain.

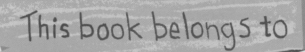

This book belongs to

....

....

ORPEN PRESS

Today is Market Day. Freddy, Ted and Kitty Buttons have a very busy day ahead.

After breakfast, the Buttons family collect produce in the garden to sell at the market.

Ted Buttons picks lots of tasty vegetables like carrots, peas and potatoes.

Kitty Buttons gathers eggs from the chickens and ducks. Then she collects apples in the orchard.

Freddy is in charge of picking the strawberries.
He goes to the strawberry patch with Juno his dog,
to pick the juiciest strawberries he can find.

Soon the Buttons' car is filled with lots of fresh produce from the garden.

And the Buttons family set off for the city.

At the market, all the producers are very busy setting up their stalls.

Mr Brody the baker and his wife are busy displaying their breads.

Greta's stall has cheese from all over the world.

Freddy and Juno can't wait to have sausages for tea tonight!

Mrs Swan sings her favourite songs while she sets out her delicious cakes and buns.

Stan the fishmonger has the freshest fish to sell today.

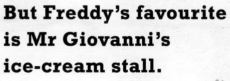

But Freddy's favourite is Mr Giovanni's ice-cream stall.

The Buttons family are all ready for a very busy day.

Soon the market is full of happy customers.

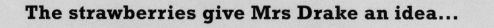

The strawberries give Mrs Drake an idea...

With these strawberries I could bake a very fine cake for next week's baking competition. Can you help Freddy?

Of course Mrs Drake. I will be here next week with the best strawberries from Tumbledown Cottage for your cake.

The next morning, Freddy and Juno get a shock when they visit the strawberry patch.

The FBI inspect the damage. There are torn
leaves and uprooted plants everywhere.

The FBI begin to interview some likely suspects. Could it be the rabbit?

**And the little mouse doesn't seem
to have caused the trouble.**

They must think of another plan.

Those nasty grey crows
had tried to wreck the strawberry patch –
Just! For! Fun!

The FBI must act fast or there will be no strawberry plants left in the garden by the end of the week.

As the sun sets, the FBI put their plan into action. They get wooden poles and a great big net from the barn.

With night falling, the FBI get to work.

As quietly as they can, they put the wooden poles around the edges of the strawberry patch.

Then they throw the great big net over the entire patch.

The next morning Freddy and Juno wake
up to great commotion in the garden.
And what do they see?

The next Saturday, Freddy and Juno are once again collecting the finest strawberries for the market.

While Freddy is busy selling his strawberries, Mrs Drake is mixing and sifting and measuring and pouring at the baking competition.

And guess what...

Mrs Drake's cake wins first prize!

DID YOU KNOW?

Strawberries are members of the rose family
(that's why they smell so great).

The strawberry is the only fruit
with seeds on the outside.

Each strawberry has about 200 seeds.

Strawberries are considered a "superfood"
because they are so nutritious.

Strawberries have even more
Vitamin C than oranges.

Strawberries are the first fruit
to ripen in the spring.

Mrs Drake's Strawberry Sundaes
Serves two GIANT sundaes

Ingredients

6 digestive biscuits

30g butter, melted

200g strawberries

2 Glenisk organic kids' strawberry yogurts

50g Glenisk organic crème fraiche

Method

Put biscuits into a bag and hit them with a rolling pin to break into crumbs.

Pour the biscuit crumb into a bowl, then stir in melted butter.

Blend the crème fraiche with the strawberry yogurts to make a mousse.

Chop strawberries into small pieces.

Layer up biscuits, mousse and berries in big glasses.

Decorate with a strawberry piece and leave in the fridge until ready to eat.

During the summer Mrs Drake makes these for her children as a special treat. When there are no longer strawberries in the garden, she uses raspberries.